$$t(x^2) \div \sqrt{9\, y(x)} = \int b_i$$

a

b

e

h

c

$$4.729 - 1.3(x^2) \times \frac{6}{4}(y^6) = X\left(\frac{1}{3}\right)$$

c

$x = c/2$

864
792
46
420

$(x-j$

$fct \ \sqrt{6}$

$CH_2\ COOH$

0

WITHDRAWN

$$fct \ \frac{y\left(\frac{6+9}{2}\right)\frac{4}{2}-\frac{x}{3}}{r(3\times 2)+9}$$

a^3+

$b^2 = (\quad)(a^2-ab)$

B

A

6

m

tr

x)

2

First published in Great Britain in 2017
by Andersen Press Ltd.,
20 Vauxhall Bridge Road, London SW1V 2SA.
Text copyright © Kathryn White, 2017.
Illustrations copyright © Adrian Reynolds, 2017.
The rights of Kathryn White and Adrian Reynolds
to be identified as the author and illustrator of
this work has been asserted by them in accordance
with the Copyright, Designs and Patents Act, 1988.
All rights reserved. Printed and bound in Malaysia.
10 9 8 7 6 5 4 3 2 1
British Library Cataloguing in Publication Data available.
ISBN 978 1 78344 408 3

FOR ARTHUR, SYLVIA AND FRIDA KATHRYN. THREE BEAUTIFUL BABIES - K.W   FOR ARCHIE AND ELLA - A.R

THE TICKLE TEST

Kathryn White

Adrian Reynolds

It's easy to **tickle** a tall giraffe,

she'll **giggle** and gurgle
and chuckle and laugh.

And it's certainly fun

to tickle

a BEAR,
he'll jiggle and wriggle and bounce everywhere.

That **gave** me
a scare!

An octopus
loves to be tickled for sure,

but which was the arm
that I tickled before?

To tickle a tiger,
hide under
his knees,

Creep up and tickle an elephant's toes.

Beware

bottom trumpets – hold your nose!

Flamingos adore just a tickle or two
but watch out for feathers or they'll tickle you.

And how to tickle a crocodile?
This dangerous test needs timing and style.

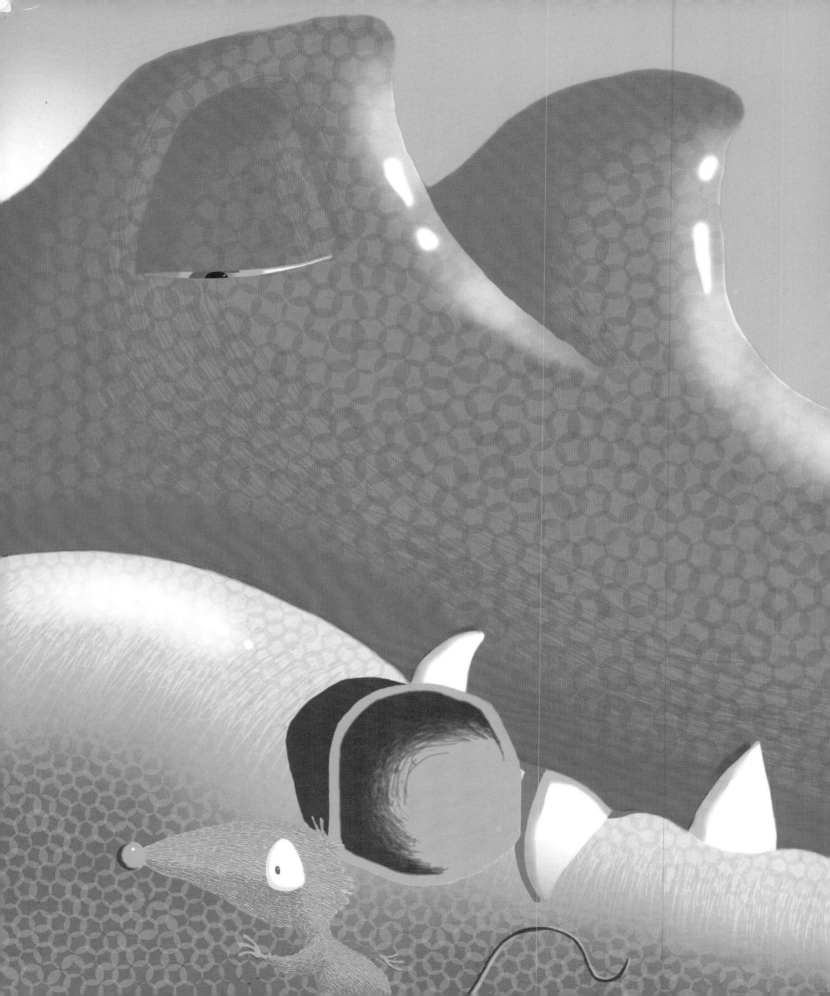

If crocodile spies you,
then you'd better dash —
those sharp teeth will
gobble you up in a flash!

he'll hoot with delight,
as he does with his mummy!
Tickling and laughing
are such fun to do.

so please tell us
just where we
should tickle...

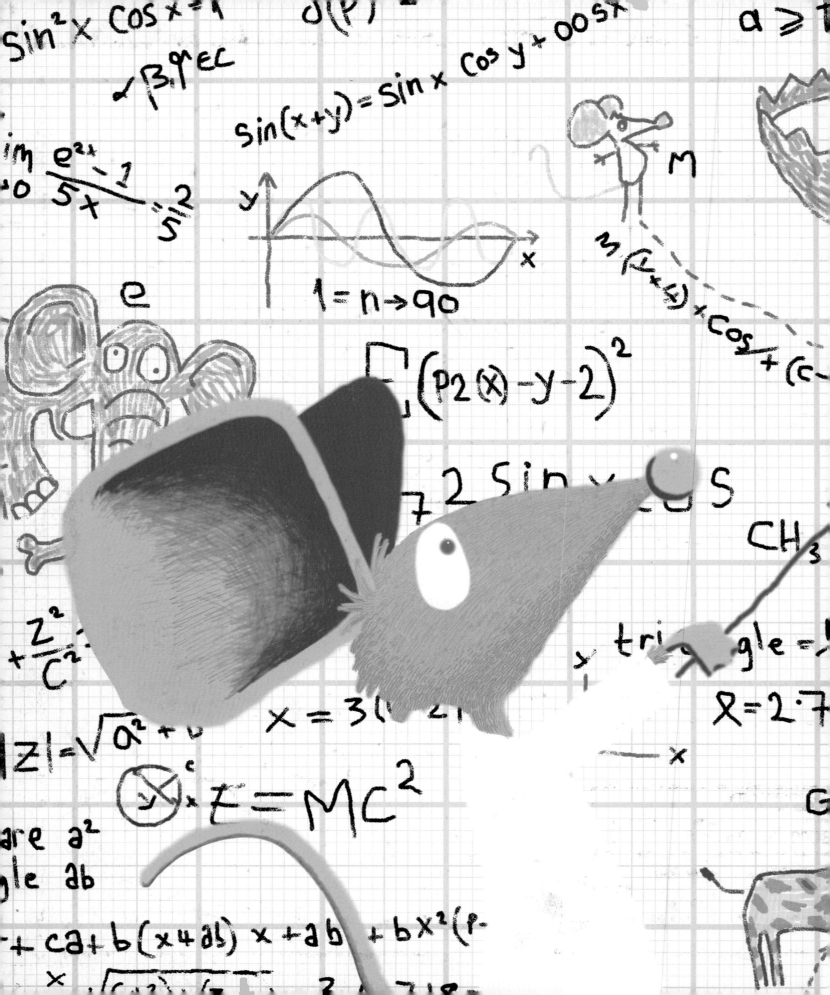

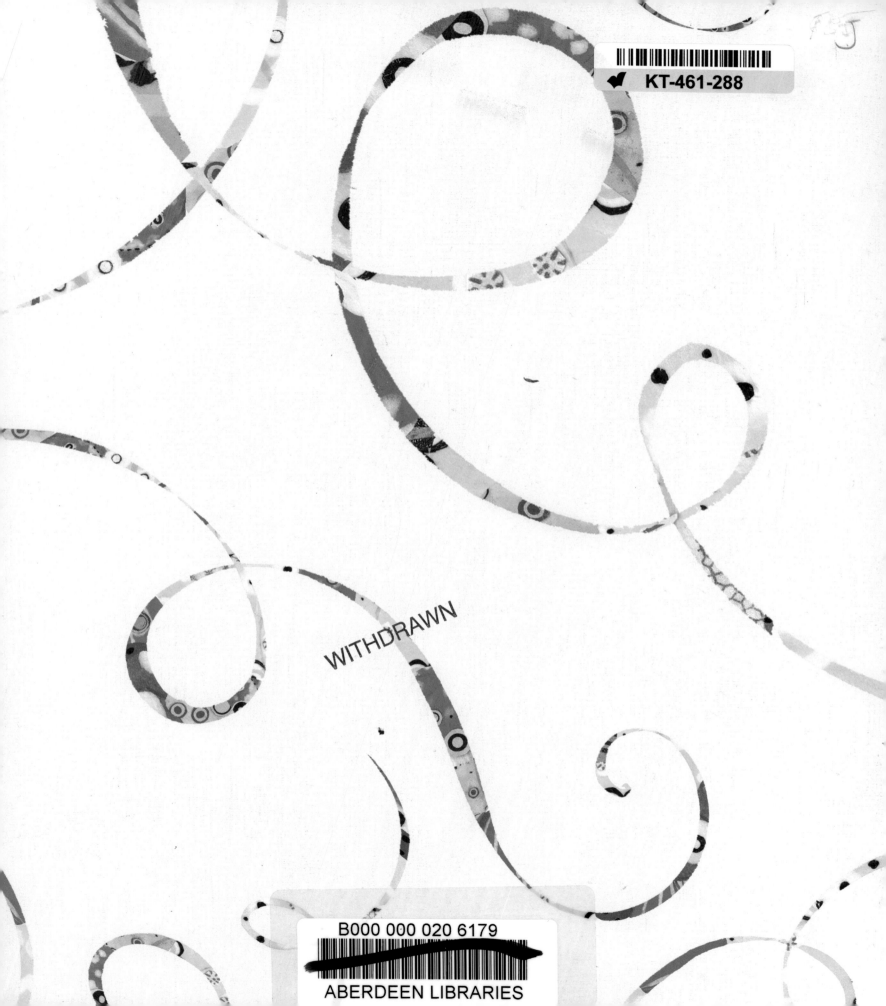

For Sonny, Johnny and Florrie

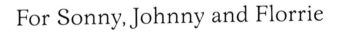

Bloomsbury Publishing, London, Oxford, New York, New Delhi and Sydney

First published in Great Britain in 2017 by Bloomsbury Publishing Plc
50 Bedford Square, London, WC1B 3DP

Text and illustrations © Suzanne Barton 2017
The moral right of the author/illustrator has been asserted

A CIP catalogue record of this book is available from the British Library

ISBN 978 1 4088 6484 5

Printed in China by C & C Offset Printing Co Ltd, Shenzhen, Guangdong

1 3 5 7 9 10 8 6 4 2

All papers used by Bloomsbury Publishing are natural, recyclable products made
from wood grown in well-managed forests. The manufacturing processes conform
to the environmental regulations of the country of origin

www.bloomsbury.com

BLOOMSBURY is a registered trademark of Bloomsbury Publishing Plc

The
Butterfly
Dance

Suzanne Barton

BLOOMSBURY
LONDON OXFORD NEW YORK NEW DELHI SYDNEY

In amongst the buzzing and humming of
summer came the steady sound of crunching.

Most of the caterpillars ate by themselves but
Dotty and Stripe shared everything.

One day, Stripe said,
"I'm so full, I think I'll
have a little sleep."

He spun himself a silky hammock
and snuggled up tight inside.

That's strange, thought Dotty.

"Wake up, sleepy head!"
she called. But there
was no answer.

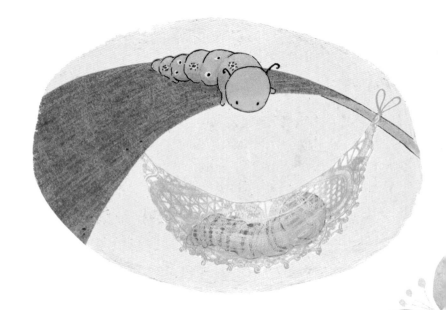

It wasn't much fun without Stripe.
They'd always done everything
together and Dotty felt lonely.

I'm a bit sleepy, too,
she thought.

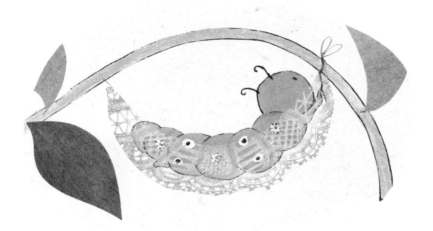

So Dotty spun herself
a cosy bed and soon
fell fast asleep.

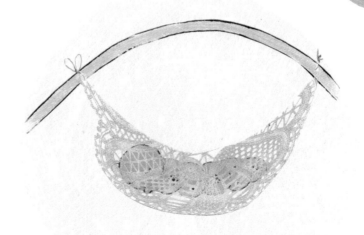

As the days passed,
Dotty's cocoon began to wiggle.
Until one morning, it cracked open . . .

. . . and she burst out into the sunshine.
Dotty blinked and gasped,
"I've got wings!"

*Where's Stripe, I can't wait
to show him?!* she thought.

"Dotty!" called a dazzling butterfly gliding down beside her.

"Stripe?! Is that you?" she asked.
        "Look! You've still got your stripes!"

"And you have your dots!" said Stripe.

"What shall we do now that we're
        butterflies?" asked Dotty.

"We fly, of course!" said Stripe.
"Come on, I'll show you how . . ."

They balanced on the edge of the leaf.
"One . . . two . . . three . . ."

And they were off!

Gliding and looping . . .

soaring and whirling, fluttering and chasing.

Until raindrops sent
them diving for cover.

"I'm hungry," said Stripe.

A little bee popped out from a flower. "These bluebells are tasty but you might prefer the thistles."

"And you might like the poppies," another bee told Dotty.

"The meadow's full of flowers," they buzzed.

"Where's the meadow?" asked Dotty.

"Through the trees," buzzed the bees.

And as the rain stopped and the bees danced
away to make honey, Dotty and Stripe
fluttered off to the woods.

Stripe liked flying fast and Dotty liked flying high,
but best of all they liked flying together.

Far below, they saw a group of
dragonflies in a puddle.
"Let's go for a paddle," said Dotty,
and down they swooped.

They sipped the cool water and splashed in the mud.
"Are you looking for the other red butterflies?" said
a dragonfly. "They're down by the thistles."

"Others?" said Dotty.

"Maybe there are other butterflies that look
like me. Let's find out," said Stripe.

They fluttered through the gentle breeze until they spotted some ladybirds. Dotty asked, "Have you seen any other butterflies like us?"

"Do you mean the little blue ones?" replied a friendly ladybird. "They're playing in the poppies."

"Oh!" said Dotty. "There must be some butterflies that look like me!"

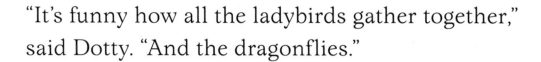

"It's funny how all the ladybirds gather together," said Dotty. "And the dragonflies."

"And the bees," said Stripe. "Maybe I'm supposed to play with butterflies that look like me?"

"And I'm supposed to play with the ones that look like me?" said Dotty.

They had never been apart before – they were BEST friends.

They sat together for a long while, and then the two friends said goodbye.

Stripe found the red butterflies
playing hide-and-seek.

"Please can I play, too?"
he asked.

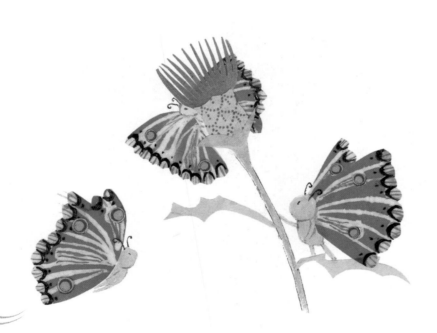

He had a great time,
but he missed Dotty.

It just wasn't the same
without her.

Dotty joined the blue butterflies
dancing among the poppies.

She had fun but wished
Stripe were there, too.

"I miss my friend," Dotty said to one
of the blue butterflies. "But I can't be
with him anymore. He's with the other
red butterflies, in the thistles."

"It's only because they love the taste of
thistles!" said the butterfly. "You can
still play with your friend. Come on,
I've got something to show you . . . !"

And off they flew until they came to . . .

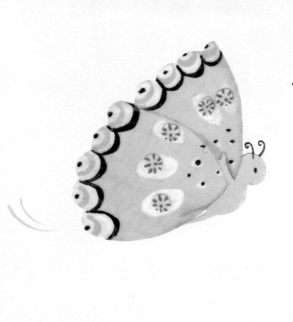

. . . the meadow.

"Wow!" said Dotty. "So many friends,
and they're all playing together!"

But how will I ever find Stripe? thought Dotty.

Then, at the edge of the crowd, she spotted
a butterfly, hovering all alone.

Dotty darted across
the meadow . . .

"Stripe!" she called.
"I missed you!"

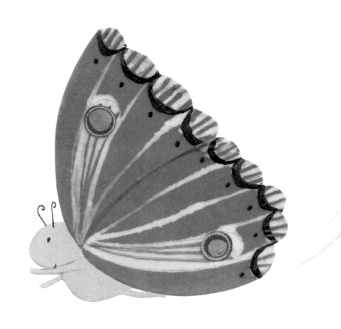

"And I missed you!"
said Stripe.

And, as the sun went down, they flew off to join in the wild dance.